Modern Curriculum Press

BEGINNING
TO
READ
Series

Sydney Taylor

THE DOG WHO CAME TO DINNER

Illustrated by John E. Johnson

MODERN CURRICULUM PRESS

ISBN: 0-8136-5543-9
Printed in the United States of America

10 11 12 13 14 15   06 05 04 03 02

Modern
Curriculum
Press

Pearson Learning Group

1-800-321-3106
www.pearsonlearning.com

$\mathbf{M}$r. Brown looked at the
empty house next door.

"That house has been empty
for a long time," he said.

"Yes," said Mrs. Brown.

"And it is such a nice house, too.
I wish some nice family
would move into it."

"A family with a girl," said Jane.

"A family with a boy," said Jimmy.

But no one moved in.

One day the Brown family went on
a trip.

When they came home, Mr. Brown cried,

"Look! There is a new mailbox on
the fence next door!"

Jimmy ran to look.

"The name on the box is Lane!"

"Oh, how nice!" said Mrs. Brown.

"Someone has moved into the empty house!"

"We must make them feel at home," said Mr. Brown.

"Yes," said Mrs. Brown.

"I will ask them to come to our house for dinner."

That night when Mr. Brown
opened the door —
In came Mr. and Mrs. Lane.
In came Peter and Peggy Lane.
And
IN CAME A BIG DOG!

"How do you do?" said Mr. Brown.

"How do you do?" said Mr. and
Mrs. Lane.

"It was nice of you to ask us
to dinner."

"We are glad to have you," said
Mrs. Brown.

"Dinner will be ready soon."

They all went into the living
room and sat down.

Mr. and Mrs. Brown talked to
Mr. and Mrs. Lane.

Jimmy Brown talked to Peter Lane.

Jane Brown talked to Peggy Lane.

The big dog ran round and round
the room.

He ran to Mr. Brown.

"Ark! Ark!" he barked.

Mr. Brown patted him.

"Nice dog," he said.

The dog ran to Mrs. Brown.

He put his front paws in her lap.

"Oh!" cried Mrs. Brown, laughing.

Then the dog ran to Mrs. Lane.

He wagged his tail.

Mrs. Lane patted him.

"Nice dog," she said.

Next the dog ran to Mr. Lane.

He sniffed at Mr. Lane's shoes.

Then he chewed on the shoes.

Mr. Lane pulled his feet away.

Now the dog ran to Jane.

He tried to jump into her lap.

His wet tongue licked her face.

Jane laughed.

Peggy tried to stand up.

The dog jumped up to lick
her face, too.

Peggy fell down on top of Jane.

Everyone laughed.

The big dog seemed to be laughing, too.

He ran round and round and tried to catch his tail.

Soon he ran to Peter and Jimmy.

He jumped all over them and licked their faces.

"He likes to play," said Peter.

"Yes," Jimmy said.

"See how his tail is wagging."

Now the dog smelled something nice.

He poked his nose into the candy dish.

Crunch! He chewed some candy.

Crunch! Crunch!

He chewed some more candy.

He ran to another nice smell.

He poked his nose into the cookie dish.

Crunch! He chewed on a cookie.

Crunch! Crunch!

He chewed on some more cookies.

The children laughed.

"He likes sweets!" they cried.

Mr. and Mrs. Brown did not like it.

They looked at Mr. and Mrs. Lane.

But they did not say anything.

They were too polite.

Mr. and Mrs. Lane looked at
Mr. and Mrs. Brown.

But they did not say anything.

Then Mrs. Brown said,

"Dinner is ready."

They all went into the dining
room and sat down.

The big dog went into the dining
room, too.

But he did not sit down.

He ran round and round the room.

He put his front paws on the table
and sniffed at Mr. Lane's plate.

He poked his nose into Mrs. Lane's plate.

His wet tongue washed Jane's plate.

His front paws went all over Jimmy's plate.

He wagged his tail.

Mr. and Mrs. Brown did not like it.

They looked at Mr. and Mrs. Lane.

But they did not say anything.

They were too polite.

Mr. and Mrs. Lane did not tell
the dog to stop.

They looked at Mr. and Mrs. Brown.

But they did not say anything.

Then Mr. Brown said very politely,

"What is the name of your dog?"

"Our dog?" said Mr. Lane.

"He is not our dog!" cried Mrs. Lane.

"Oh!" said Mr. and Mrs. Brown.

"But he came in with you!" Jane said.

"He was standing in front of your house," Peter said.

"So we thought he was your dog!" cried Peggy.

"Our dog?" said Mr. Brown.

"He is not our dog!" cried Mrs. Brown.

"Oh!" said Mr. and Mrs. Lane.

Then Mrs. Brown said,
"He is not your dog.
He is not our dog.
Whose dog is he?"
"He must belong to
someone!" Jimmy cried.
"He has a collar."

Mr. Brown looked at the collar.

"He lives on the next block."

"Why did he come to our house?"
asked Jane.

"He wants to make some new
friends, too," said Mrs. Lane.

"So he came to dinner," said Mrs. Brown.

Everyone laughed and laughed.

The dog barked and wagged his tail.

"The dog poked his nose into
all our plates," said Mrs. Brown.

"Come Jane, we must wash them.

Then we will have our dinner."

"And the dog, too?" cried the children.

"Yes," said Mr. Brown.

"The dog will have some dinner, too."

When dinner was over, they all went
into the living room and sat down.

"It was such a nice dinner,
Mrs. Brown," said Mrs. Lane.

"I am glad you liked it,"
said Mrs. Brown.

"Ark! Ark!" barked the dog.

"He liked the dinner, too,"
said Peggy.

"Yes," said Peter.

"See how his tail is wagging."

The dog ran to the door.

He put his front paws on it.

"Ark! Ark!" he barked.

Jimmy said, "Dinner is over.

Now he wants to go home."

Everyone laughed and laughed.

The dog seemed to be laughing, too.

He barked again and wagged
his tail.

Mr. Brown opened the door.

The dog who came to dinner
ran all the way home.

THE DOG WHO CAME TO DINNER

The Dog Who Came to Dinner has a total vocabulary of 181 words. Regular possessives and contractions (*-'s, -n't, -'ll, -'m*), regular verb forms (*-s, -ed, -ing*), and regular plurals (*-s*) of words already on the list are not listed separately, but the endings are given in parentheses after the words.

5 Mr.	a	I	one
Brown	long	wish	in
look (ed)	time	some	day
at	he	family	went
the	said	would	on
empty	yes	move (d)	trip
house	Mrs.	into	when
next	and	**6** with	they
door	it	girl	came
that	is	Jane ('s)	home
has	such	Jimmy ('s)	cried
been	nice	but	there
for	too	no	new

mailbox
fence
7 ran
to
name
box
Lane ('s)
oh
how
someone
we
must
make
them
feel
will
ask
come
our
dinner
8 night
opened
Peter
Peggy
big
dog
9 do
you
was
of
us
are
glad

have
be
ready
soon
10 all
living
room
sat
down
talked
round
11 barked
patted
him
put
his
front
paws
her
lap
laugh (ing) (ed)
12 then
wagged
tail
sniffed
shoes
chewed
pulled
feet
away
13 now
tried

jump (ed)
wet
tongue
lick (ed)
face (s)
stand
up
fell
top
everyone
14 seemed
catch
over
their
15 like (s) (ed)
play
see
wagging
smelled
something
poked
nose
candy
dish
crunch
more
16 another
smell
cookie
children
sweets
17 did

not
say
anything
were
polite
18 dining
19 sit
table
plate
wash (ed)
20 tell
stop
21 very
politely
what
your
22 was
standing
so
thought
23 whose
belong
collar
24 lives
block
why
wants
friends
26 am
27 go
28 who
way

31